Wake Up a Woman

Laura A. Lord

Wake Up a Woman

"Turning Out the Light" and "Over-Loved"
were previously published in *The Beacon*.

"It Was Winter" was previously published in *Whirl with Words*

ISBN: 978-0-9833159-7-1

Art: Magic Meadow by Aleshyn Andrei

Public Domain

Second Printing

CHESTER RIVER PRESS
Chestertown, Maryland
www.chesterriverpress.com

2012
Chester River Press
Fine Printing & Publishing

For my amazing, beautiful children.
You are the best part of me.

Table of Contents

Wake Up a Woman

WAKE UP A WOMAN

I went to bed a child

In footie pajamas.

I scrunched my feet across the carpet,

Static shot from my fingertips

And I shocked the World.

I woke with the sun set.

I woke with the sky dark.

I woke and God had pulled his blanket

Across the sky.

He blotted out the moon.

He laughs at me.

The booming sound echoes across the landscape.

It rattles the window panes.

It shakes the foundations.

I stole His thunder.

I stole His lightning.

I had no static left,

So I made it mine.

And I shocked the World.

I shocked the World.

I am not who he made.

I went to bed a child,

My footie pajamas torn,

Bare feet hanging through and scraping

Across cold, tiled floors.

I lost my static.

Wake up a woman.

GOURMET MEALS

She's angry. I mean, she is pissed beyond belief. It's Christmas time and her face is the same shade of red as the shining balls on the tree. She's screaming in that high pitched, whiny voice I thought only young boys and teenage girls were capable of. Except, she's twenty, too old for this.

The TV her parents got her, wrapped in glittering silver paper and topped with a silky bow, is not the right TV. It's not the one she asked for, and she is…unhappy, to say the least.

Suddenly, it's seven years ago, and I'm sitting on a picnic table in the park, watching the puny fire that's cooking my stolen dinner. Ever had frozen pizzas on the grill? I watch the bottom of it blacken and the cheese stay in the same frozen strips across the top. He's around here somewhere, scrounging for firewood in a State Park that doesn't allow people to cut down its trees. The pile of pine needles we've scooped up for kindling is almost as high as the tent. The wood stack isn't even a stack. It's a row of three or four pieces, soaking wet and half rotten.

My stomach growls and that half-burnt, half-frozen pizza is looking better every minute. I search for one of the two plates we have and pry the gourmet meal off the grill top with a stick. He's been gone for a while now, and I can't hear the normal rustling sounds of his feet through the leaves.

A dog would turn his head from this pizza. He'd back away from it like it carried some sort of disease, turn up his nose, and search for a trashcan that was sure to hold better pickings. I eat it anyway, and it's better than the almost constant meal of catfish. Better even than the days we don't catch any fish.

This is our tenth night paying the daily rent for our little square of gravel and brush, our Marlboro Man tent, our picnic table, and grill. Ten nights of showering in the bathroom stalls, of carrying buckets of water from the pump to drink. Ten nights of mosquitoes and spiders the size of my hand. Ten nights of embracing the cold so we wouldn't have to touch one another.

The TV is two sizes smaller than she wanted. It won't look right in her new bedroom. It's too tiny for the huge space on the wall she left open to hang it. What a shame.

It's my grandmother's funeral today. I'm in a stall at the park, with dirt on the floor and cobwebs hanging from the ceiling like streamers. I'm slipping on the one nice dress I have with me, and wishing it wasn't so wrinkly from its time in the garbage bag of my closet. It's almost a size too big now, and we didn't catch any fish this morning.

He doesn't come with me, so I'm there, with all my family and my grandmother's one-million friends, and I'm alone. Everyone tells me how pretty I am, but they don't stand close enough to know I'm not wearing any deodorant, and I have no idea where my make-up is. They don't know I washed up in a sink this morning. They think that's the piano playing but it's really my stomach growling. I need a cigarette, and I know Daddy will give me one, but I hate to ask him for anything else. Last week he gave me a box of food. He cried and I walked away, because I couldn't comfort him. I didn't know how. So I cried. There weren't arms big enough to comfort us both, not then.

She's still yelling about the TV and I'm sitting under the twinkling lights on the banister, laughing my head off. This huge grin covers my face and I laugh until tears well in my eyes. I laugh until the room spins and the presents are gone. I laugh until that "Have A Holly Jolly Christmas" song is gone, replaced by the soft swishing of leaves falling through branches. I laugh until the heat from the fireplace turns into that of a meek, little campfire. I laugh until Christmas is gone and I'm in the park, sitting on my picnic table and waiting for my gourmet meal.

KNEEL

They taught me about God. They taught me about Heaven and Hell, Angels and Demons. They taught me how to bow my head, how to kneel.

I'm standing in this open doorway and the walls are bare and the floors are a solid brick of concrete. There's a rug, some perverted exercise at decoration. It's not even raining, but I scrub my feet across it again and again in some vain effort to wipe away the sludge I carry with me. I stand there for a minute, for a year, wiping my feet against the rough surface of that rug as I watch it turn filthy underneath me.

There's only about a million folding, metal chairs in the room and I'd sit but I've forgotten how to kneel. So I stand there, a welcome stranger, as he hands them the cash. I'm in. That's it, I'm in.

She's asking me too many questions.

"Did anyone force you to come here?"

"Are you doing this of your own free will?"

I ask her if she saw Him? Did she see His face? I have no Devil on my left. He's on my right. He's in front of me and behind me. He's under me and over me. He's inside me. He's pulling the strings and I'm just along for the ride.

I cling to my Angel like a life raft, but still the rapids wash over me. Still the water floods my mouth and I'm standing here drowning in front of her. I'm choking for air and clinging to my Angel, who is a rock in my belly, a boulder I couldn't begin to carry, and it's dragging me down, but still I clasp myself to it.

She takes my blood and I look at the vial and it's empty. I suppose this is what she wanted. "Patient is empty. She's numb. The patient is ready for you, Doctor." She takes out a needle the size of Texas, and I feel nothing, but I know I can't sit. I forgot how to kneel.

"Ba-bump. Ba-bump. Ba-bump." It is the sound of my Angel. I can see him on the screen and they look at it. I look at it. The whole world looks at it for that moment and then, with a flick of a switch, it's gone.

I'm on my back, without the slightest illusion of clothing to cover me and she's telling me to breathe. Her hands are fists on my shoulders, her chest laid across mine and she wants me to breathe. I can't breathe. She's smothering me. I look down and see my stomach collapsing into itself. I'm eating myself whole and vomiting who I used to be back across the floor.

"Breathe. You have to breathe."

Can't she see my body is failing? I bow my head, because it's all I can remember how to do. My body is twisting in on itself; it's folding and crumpling into a phantom of what I was.

"It'll be over in a minute. Breathe."

My lungs burn, but I can't breathe. I can't open my mouth, and I can't kneel. When she's off me I can see the blood. I see it everywhere. They've decorated the room with my soul. They've hung it like curtains from the non-existent windows. They've turned it into the fibers of a plush carpet. They've set it out like a welcome mat.

She gives me Goldfish crackers and pills to swallow, and I do. I watch them slip and fall out of the hole that was my belly. I watch them hit the floor and flop around, as I hum the Goldfish tune. I watch them swim away and I follow them out, out the door, down the hall, onto the street. I follow them to the trashy hotel where there are more bugs in the quilts than stitches.

He's lying across the bed, a bottle of Southern Comfort in His hands.

Don't you care they just took my Angel?

"When can we fuck?"

I stare at Him like he spoke another language. I stand in the doorway, my back against the cool metal, because I've forgotten how to kneel. I bow my head. I can still, always, bow my head.

The Demon isn't on my left. He's on my right. He's in front of me and behind me. He's over me and under me. He's on top of me and inside me.

A crack like a gunshot slams the room. My legs pop and break. My body folds into itself as He dives away from me. He looks at me as if I am a stranger.

"Who are you?"

Who am I?

My knees rub against the sandpaper carpet. I beg. I cry. I plead. I kneel.

TURNING OUT THE LIGHT

Let me start out by saying, I am a resilient person. That is to say that in fact, I am a moron. I am a stubborn woman, who allows the same negative garbage in my life to continue to walk all over me. At least that is, until I find my proverbial "nuts" and I am finally able to gather the strength to crawl out of my newest mess. Sounds crazy, doesn't it? Insanity is described as doing the same thing again and again and expecting a different result. I can truly say that I have a firm grip on this insanity. I completely understand it, and revert to it on an almost casual basis.

I say all that to say this, Tank and I were a pair in insanity. We fit together like a moth and a porch light. He was the attractive one, and I was simply banging my head into him again and again without much more result than a splitting headache. I walked out on Tank three times, and I can say, I am a professional packer. Truly I can have a team of family members, trucks, and boxes, and be out of the house in less than two hours. No one could find a stray sock to remember me by, I swear. However, leaving is painful. It was painful in the physical sense, for I certainly experienced serious back pain from all the heavy box lifting. Moreover, my life was never quite the same again. Those very same boxes, packed with all the same belongings, are heavy with the sludgy residue of grief and regrets. We were certainly filled with grief. Tank was my best friend, and I was his. We had made each other our "everything," which meant that when all was said and done, we left with nothing.

Our "everything" began in a completely destructive nature. We were two relative strangers, who rushed into a relationship with one another and who fell rather hard into that black hole called "Love." Naturally, the next step in any relationship of this caliber is to have a child, and the first time I left was after we saw that adorable blue plus sign. This isn't to say that our son wasn't wanted, or even talked away, but just another point to show our moronic and hormone-induced decision-making processes. Since we were already making such wonderful decisions, we quickly decided to come back together and find a place of our own to call home. We moved into a tiny, run-down trailer a few months later. I remember it fondly; the carpet was brown shag, and my daughter's room was the size of a closet, literally. It was our first home, and we were so excited to bring our new son into it. He was beautiful, healthy, and completely exhausting. Two weeks, and hardly any sleep later, Tank was squealing tires out of the gravel drive, while I loaded a newborn and my daughter into a tiny, little Focus, crammed to the ceiling with random pillows, t-shirts, and Elmo toys, for yet another move home. That evening Tank called me, and while we were both in emotional ruins, it was I who had to offer him the comforting words he needed so badly to hear. The words seeped out of me coated in bitter anger at the fact that I was the one who had been hurt so badly, and yet still I braced myself for more pain and held him up once more.

The whole moving home thing lasted about three weeks, but the betrayal and pain had a firm foothold on us by then. Before I knew it we were making more insane decisions, and signed a lease on a much bigger house, busying ourselves with renovations. You see, the house wasn't quite ready to live in, not with the wooden shelves in the fridge and the large gaping holes in the ceilings. I will say that the mice were very creative in the places they chose to die, as it was always an enjoyable moment to have one randomly fall onto my feet from the swinging cabinet door. The colorful children's graffiti added a nice touch in the bedrooms, though I will always be puzzled as to how the crayon made its way onto the ceiling.

Before long the renovations were done, and we were happily moving into our new home. Fresh new carpet sprung back under our feet in that not-so-pretty brown color anyone with young children tends to pick out as a "safe" one. Here in our new home, Tank and I were happy. I can remember one of our first nights, after waiting until the children were sleeping quietly in their beds; we took an old blanket outside and spread it on the ground behind the worn-out, red barn. Tank and I laid there for hours, and I can still hear his voice saying to me, "Remember when we did this at your house and your Dad came out? I thought for sure he'd find us." For those few moments it was like it used to be between us and our laughter filled the late night air.

Those first days in October were the few nice memories of that home that I have, and not-so-surprisingly, by February a moving crew was backing up to the house. The morning was spent hurling names and casting blame, arguing and yelling to see who could deliver the most painful blow. I have to say, Tank always had a knack for that. I remember keeping my head down low, hoping some of the jabs would ping off the wall behind me, until finally his truck shot down the driveway.

That evening, I came back for the few boxes of Christmas things left in the basement. Tank sat there, in the damp, badly lit basement, and cried. With barely concealed pain I remembered all of the time he had hurt me. For the last time his unfaithfulness and lies had pushed me to pack up my children and move away. I remembered that each of those times, it was me who had to comfort him in the painful aftermath. With perfect clarity I can see him sitting there, crushing some flimsy cardboard box beneath him, his face buried in his hands. I remember turning my back and walking up the steps, the sound of tiny metal ornaments clanking together in the box in my hands. My feet were lead blocks on the creaking steps, and my stomach was jogging a slow lope up into my throat. I had left Tank many times. but that was the first time I ever walked away from him.

For weeks my phone rang and I knew on the other end was a drunk voice, clogged with anger, regrets, and grief. Sometimes I answered it, and I tried to be the woman he needed me to be. I tried once again to be the friend, the companion. I tried to take the blame and to listen to him as he spilled his grief over me. Except that grief poured over me like sour milk. I couldn't be that girl anymore. Perhaps we were both resilient, too much so. Both of us were moronic little moths, slamming into the light again and again.

I know that sometimes having someone in my life involves holding him up when he is down. However, if I am the only one doing the holding, eventually my arms are going to get tired. Things will happen in life that will bring me to my knees, but the important thing is to know that I have someone there who can lift me back up. I remember all this with pain and with hope. I moved on, slowly, but steadily. I enrolled in college, got a job, or two or three. I met someone amazing, whose arms seem to never tire and who reaches out for me just as often as I do him. As for Tank, I have no idea what became of him. That friendship was lost in the rubble of the relationship, which in all aspects, is probably for the best. It was past time for someone to turn out the light.

PERFECT SQUARES

I hated that woodstove. I hated the way the grass and dirt from the yard clung to my feet in the early morning when I would run to the wood pile. I hated the splinters that littered my forearms and fingers from the chunks of broken trees. I hated that no matter how high the fire was stoked it never warmed my kitchen. And yet, the living room, where that fire blazed, was so hot I could barely stand to sit in there for more than a few moments at a time. More than the cold, early mornings and the fine splinters, more than anything, I hated that smoky film that layered every surface of the house.

Freshly painted walls were bright white. It never lasted long, especially once winter came and the woodstove was roaring to life. The walls never stood a chance. Black smoke trickled into the rooms, staining the walls and leaving bits of ash and dust over every single surface. I vacuumed every single day. Thankfully the carpet was a horrendous brown shade that seemed to absorb even the ash from the wood. Every day I dusted. I grabbed my cloth and sprayed and wiped until the entire house smelled like lemons, and still that yellowish stain spread across my home like a disease.

I only lived in that old farmhouse for a few months. It was far from the cheery place I had envisioned it would be. The yard was littered with dilapidated buildings and empty patches where grass just would not grow. The concrete steps were cracked and broken; they had left chunks of their stone draped across the front yard like some kind of plea to be noticed. The porch sagged at such an angle that my children's' toys would simply roll off it and get lost in the tall grass beneath.

The upstairs was probably the worst. Wallpaper that was God-only-knows how many years old hung in ribbons from the walls. The floors were bare and cold, because even with the woodstove below raging and sputtering its debris, the heat never reached our bedroom. The room was a perpetual icebox; so cold in fact, that the memory foam mattress had frozen, the imprint of our bodies stamped in relief on its surface. I remember looking at it and thinking that it was lucky we had gotten such a large bed. Two people could not have possibly gotten any more space between them than we had.

He was never home. I spent my days there with the children. I vacuumed and dusted and alternated between the sweltering heat of the living room and the frozen expanse of the kitchen. Occasionally he'd be there when we ate a meal, but setting a place for him was more like an afterthought. He didn't belong there with us. He didn't belong to that house. I belonged to it. Everything I did, every single day, was dictated by that house. I blamed him for it, and my hatred of that place caused an ever widening chasm between us. I mean, the longer we were there, the less attached I felt to him. It felt as if slowly that yellowish film that coated all of my possessions, even my beautiful white walls, was smothering me. Then he would walk in and it never touched him. The house wanted me too much to waste its time touching him.

Leaving that house was easier than staying. I remember boxes scattered around every room, my mother dumping clothes from the closets into them and my father hauling out the random pieces that made up my life. I remember we had a wall of photos. I'd hung them right after we moved in. I was so proud of myself, using a hammer and nails, and positioning everything so straight, all by myself. The photographs took up the entire wall. I saw myself, my children, my family, even my cats. There was one there with him in it, but it was new. I'd just hung it up a few days ago. I pulled all the rest of them off and stacked them in the boxes, but I left his picture there. Let the house have him now.

I brought the kids back to see him and they stood there, strangers in what had been their home for a short while. We stood in the doorway to the living room, the cold air from the kitchen hitting our backs and the blaze from the woodstove searing our faces. He was there by that wall, scrubbing at it. He was so determined in his work; I don't think he even knew we were there. When I came closer I saw the squares. Perfect, white squares were scattered across the wall, surrounded by that ugly yellow stain that had covered everything. "I just can't get it all clean. That yellow stuff is everywhere. I can't get it off." It was wrong, and yet, I smiled. I couldn't even help myself. The house hadn't destroyed everything. Every place where a photograph of my family had been was as perfect as it had been on the day we first arrived.

I didn't belong to that house anymore. We'd gotten out of it. The only parts of us that hadn't been destroyed by that damned stove were gone. I left him stronger. I could chop and carry wood. I could repair drywall, lay tile, put down carpeting, and fix concrete. I could walk away from that house, that stove. I left him, scrubbing at the walls, trying to rid himself of the memories that I had made there, the impression I had left behind.

STILL WAITING

My phone buzzes and vibrates; it lights up and winks in and out to a silenced tune. It somehow seems to leap across my pillow and into my hand, so I wake and see his picture. My eyes, still stuck with the night-time glue, see him first, his smiling face and grey-blue eyes, blinking in and out of the darkness. It takes a moment, only a brief one, before I'm up and on my feet. With the light from my phone I check my shadowy reflection in the mirror.

I went to bed dressed for the event.

I stub my toe on the rolling wheel of my bed as I fight to pull the blanket free. It's a huddle of cloth and fuzz in my arms as I slip out of the slightly creaking door and down the hallway.

I see a light flashing from the big bay window in the front.

With a quick peek behind me, to be sure I am still alone, I pry the door open. It squeaks on its hinges, but thankfully doesn't stick. I'm out the door. I'm gone: my blanket and I.

He's there when I lay the blanket down, hidden behind the huge shed in my yard. He's looking better than his picture did, flashing on my phone. For now though, I ignore him. I'm on my hands and knees pulling at the corners and attempting to get the blanket down flat.

But it won't go flat, because the land's too bumpy.

He could help, but he won't. He keeps his distance. The only hint of his presence is the fiery end of his cigarette. It swirls through the darkness, cutting a path of orange as grey smoke pools around him, as if he needed more shadows here to cover his face.

I'm still on my knees and my back is to him. The blanket is as straight as it's going to get, but I can't leave it alone. It's not perfect. It used to lay flat here. It used to.

He's in his uniform: green and gold, pointed and roped. Medals clink and clang against one another as he shifts his arm and takes another drag off his cigarette. So I light one up now and turn to him. I plop onto the blanket, my legs spread open and knees up. I'm resting my arms and my head on those knees. As long as I'm smoking I don't have to smile and as long as I'm trying not to smile it won't hurt if I cry.

He flicks the butt away and kneels down in the gap between my legs. He doesn't bother to take off his hat, his cover. It's a cover. I sit back a bit then, opening myself up to him.

He grasps my cigarette and throws it out.

So I'm out of excuses. Not that it mattered; it could only last for so long anyway. His eyes are dead and my heart is empty. We make love until the bruises in our souls show bright on our skin. He turns me into a blanket to warm the chill out of his heart and I take nothing from him but his time, just a few more moments.

"Just a few more minutes."

My pleas mean nothing, and he lights another cigarette. He's lying back, away from me, and I'm on my side looking at him. My fingers trail across his jacket and one-by-one I pluck the medals off. I yank them with swift fingers so they tear the fabric. I crush them in my hands and throw them into the trees. I'm screaming now as I tear them and blood begins to run. I'm pulling them free and they're stuck to his chest. They pop free with sickening, flesh rending sounds. I squeeze them between my fingers until they are gold powder on my palm, until the blood mixes with them and the gold makes it shine.

He hands me the short off his cigarette and stands up.

I let the cigarette fall out of my hand. It hits the blanket and the old thing goes up in flames around me. I'm kneeling in the middle of that fire, screaming as my hair falls off in wisps of ash and my nightgown melts to my skin.

He rubs a thumb across one of his medals, brushing a bit of cigarette ash off its shiny front.

"Wait for me. I'll be back in a few months. You'll see."

Wait for him.

Wait for him.

I'm still waiting.

LAUGHING WITH GOD

I bow my head.

I clasp my hands.

I hit my knees.

I laugh.

Scratch that.

Quickly!

Before the Book-thumping,

Holes-In-Their-Rollers,

Sorta women

Roll me

Flat, flat, flat.

I believe in their God.

I believe He has a sense of humor.

Who else could have made the platypus?

The okapi?

The hairless mole-rat?

Me?

Who else could have made me?

There isn't enough correction tape in the world

To cover the words I've done,

The deeds I've wrote.

Scratch that!

Scratch that with enough ink to cover,

A blanket to drown out

My smile, my laugh.

I believe in their God.

Who else could have made me?

SPIRITUAL

The closest thing I have to a spiritual experience anymore is a Mocha Frappe from McDonald's.

I'm feeling a little empty, like there are a ton of little holes poked in me and everything is leaking out.

I'm feeling like I need a strong drink, or a cigarette, or some other vice to fill up those holes.

I need something for people to be upset with me for, so they'll stop getting upset over nothing.

I need to find my tongue, because I think I left it behind with my will. They've all run off for a ménage à trois with my strength. It may just be some freaky kind-of foursome as soon as my patience catches up with the rest of the pack.

I just finished a story, and I compared myself to a teddy bear with its stuffing falling out. At the moment, some lovely, evil child is squeezing me so hard my button eyes are about to pop off. The velvet on my nose is worn away to the plastic and there isn't any fluff left in my arms and legs.

I'm not depressed. I'm not. And I'm not in denial, even though I continue to say I'm not, as if those mere words would convince anyone.

I'm tired.

I'm also the Queen of Understatements.

OVER-LOVED

It's six o'clock in the morning and I'm wide awake. The only noise I hear is that of my boyfriend's heavy breathing next to me. His hot breath washes across the back of my neck in little puffs. Gently, I unfold myself from his arms, slip out the door and let it close behind me with a squeak. I have a few moments to myself, and even though I quit smoking months ago, I go outside and sit on the steps and breathe in the cold, wet morning air. It's only a few minutes to myself, a few precious minutes until, "Mommy, I'm awake."

The miniature tornado that is my son, the devastator with the bright grin on his face, is awake and at the door. I smile, come inside and begin my day.

First things first, and I'm searching the floor, behind the couches, under the table, on every single shelf, until I find whatever specific truck he's looking for this morning. I find it and hand it to him, and finally the bottom lip is sucked back into his smile, and he's racing off to perform stunts and crashes on my dining room table. For the moment he is occupied, and I'm in the kid's bedroom, looking at my daughter, who has yanked the covers over her head and is already whining.

"It's time to get up."

She grumbles, whines, and rolls over, the blanket crunched in her fists and hiding everything but the wispy tangles of hair that poke out around her pillow. They have a metal closet. One of those annoying loud ones that you can't open without making a huge racket. So I'm opening it, and pulling out outfits, and the little terror of a toddler is back in the room. I pull out a shirt for him and he tells me that he wants a car shirt. I dig through the pile, show him three different shirts, before he picks the first one I showed him.

"You have school this morning. Get up, or we're going to be late."

He's stripping naked in the middle of the room, waiting for me to help him get dressed and fussing because he can't get the sleeve of his nightshirt off his hand that still has a death grip on a monster truck. I take the truck and he whines some more, until the shirt is off and I hand it back. He's laughing and saying, "I gotta butt." He's dancing around the room as she's finally peeling herself out from under the blankets, and sliding her feet to the floor.

"I don't want to wear that."

I look at her with absolute exasperation. "You haven't even seen what I picked out yet."

"I don't want that one."

Now she's whining, and I tell her to pick out her own clothes. I chase down the naked dance king and start attempting to get clothing on his booty-shaking body. At least she's awake, and she's pulling through the closet for clothes that she likes, which look remarkably like the outfit I picked out for her.

I am patience.

Ten long minutes later of, "Help me with my socks," and "I can't find my shoes," and we're in the living room.

I'm handing out PopTarts like a prize, and turning on some sort of cartoon that will hopefully keep their attention for the few moments I need to find clothes of my own.

There's a pot of water on the stove boiling for some lumpy, instant coffee, and I don't even remember putting it there. But it's steaming and by now my boyfriend is awake, and I've forgotten to pack his lunch. So I'm pouring scalding water into a cup, and making sandwiches. I might as well make my daughter's while I'm here. I search for icepacks, and snacks, and no she can't have that one, because she had it yesterday. I'm out of ham, and I wonder if she'll notice if I use bologna.

He grabs his lunchbox, kisses me quickly and is out the door for work, and I'm still in my pajamas. I take a sip from my cup, and it's cold. It also tastes like nothing but water and I get a chunk of powder that explodes in my mouth like a miniature bomb. I forgot to stir it.

At some point I'm dressed, and so are the kids. Teeth are brushed, hair is combed, and I'm trying to find hair bows that match exactly, because otherwise it just wouldn't be right.

"No you can't bring your truck to daycare."

"You have to get your shoes on. Now."

"What do you mean you can't find them? Look."

"Please don't chase the cat."

"Your shoes are not on the ceiling. Stop looking up there."

I'm kissing her quick as my mom sits at the computer and tries to show me videos off the AOL news page. I watch a moment of one, laugh lightly, take another sip of my cold, chunky water and run out the door with my arms full of books. The twister that is my toddler is in his car-seat, and I only have to get out of the car three times to get things I forgot today. The drive to daycare only takes a few minutes, and he sings the "Bad to the Bone" song the entire way.

I am an alarm clock.

I'm in my first, or is it third, class of the day and my phone rings for the second or tenth time. My uncle has lost something, have I seen it? What time am I getting home? I need to talk to you. Can you keep a secret?

I write stories. My stories, everyone's story. People tell me their secrets, and I have to keep them, bottled up inside with all my stories, where they bounce around in their silence. I listen to everyone, and I guess I have that look. You know, that I-can-tell-her-anything look. That she-can-be-trusted look. My phone is buzzing in my pocket and it's someone else, with a new story that I'll never be able to tell.

I am a confidant.

I walk in the door and it's late. It's beyond late. My arms are loaded with books, and I'm guzzling an energy drink like my life depended on it. My mother is the only one out there waiting for me. Dishes are piled in the sink, and the rooms look like a toy store threw up all its used and broken merchandise across the carpet.

"This house is a mess. You need to get your priorities straight."

I am a maid.

I've been at school for thirteen hours today. I've slammed my head into my desk repeatedly over any number of x equals five times the square root of negative forty-eight divided by x raised to the third power. I've sat at work and helped people write their stories that they don't want to tell, and don't want to write, and I can't write them, because they aren't mine, and I'm only here to help them do it. I've read Shakespeare and Sophocles until my brain aches and I wonder why they couldn't just come and say what they mean. It's late, and I m tired of riddles.

I am a student.

I go to my kid's room, and my daughter is asleep. My son is tossing and turning, and he spies me through the crack in the door.

"You're home. Mommy you're home!"

It's a plea. In that moment I have relieved all his fears that this Monday would be different, this one she wouldn't come home. I haven't seen him since this morning when I dropped him off at daycare, and for him, the day has been never-ending. He leaps from his bed so fast, he slams his knee into the side of it. Sitting on the floor, he whines and cries and I scoop him up. I kiss his knee, and it's all better. So we lay in his bed for a moment and he cuddles against me tight, before I kiss his head and slip out of the room.

I am a doctor.

I maneuver around the headphone set attached to my boyfriend's head to give him a kiss. His eyes stay glued to the video game, but I know he loves me because he tells me he saved me some dinner in the fridge. I'm hungry, but I'd rather just lay here, and I curl up with my blankets and watch him save the world from zombies, demons, orcs.

Eventually, he turns it off and lies with me. I'm curled into the mold his body gives me, and we're comfortable enough to lay there with each other in that not-quiet silence. We'll make love later, desperately, like two people who haven't been near each other for months. We'll fight one another in it, make it a battle of wills. There is nothing easy or soft about our passion. It's a storm that washes over us, under us, around us. It fills us and drives us, until we're back into our places, and I'm settled into my spot against his body.

I am a puzzle piece.

I'm versatile. I am an electronic piece of technology. I am every untrained professional. I hold every job I never wanted. I'm material. I'm an over-loved teddy bear with the stuffing pouring out between the stitches.

I am Captain Obvious.

I am a teddy bear who spends all night being tossed all over, drowned in blankets, and rolled on. I end up sprawled on the hard floor in the morning, stepped on and ignored until bedtime again.

WHITE SHOULDERS

Have you ever noticed that there are places in this world that at certain times, and this is only every once in a while, time skips? It's like life is a record player, and in our little record are a few cracks. Oh they are nothing major, and the music still comes through, but at times, just certain times, the needle catches. It pauses there, and the music stops. Then, within seconds, it jumps over the crack and starts anew. Who knows how long those seconds are? I mean, what does time mean to God? An eternity for us is but a blink of the eye to Him.

Of course by this point my grandmother had stopped my explanation of cracks and records skipping. She had one of the sighs, the kind that let me know she was ready to come out of her silence. We were sitting there on that park bench, the kind with the curved metal back, that looks uncomfortable, but you end up melded right into it like you belong with the scrolls and dips and dives. Leaves floated around us in the colors of flaming ash, all reds, oranges and yellows. My Grandmother's cape was red. Not the red of the leaves, or a sunset over tired skies. No, her cape was the color of a fire engine. As if she should be putting out all those little flames that fell around us, and she could have too. She'd been putting out fires all of my life.

"Now stop this nonsense, and tell me what's really going on."

Her voice was one of soft strength, and as she spoke, one small, wrinkled, beautiful hand slipped out from under that cape and grasped mine. I couldn't just settle for her hand though, and instead I curled myself into her, like I'd done since I was a child. My grandmother was no twig of a woman. She was the kind of woman you hugged and instead of being afraid you might break her, you knew she was the one holding you together. She was comfortable, and as I hugged her the scent of White Shoulders chased away everything else.

It was easier to talk now, so I told her of school and how well it was going. I talked about my professors and how much support they have given me in my writing. I spoke of work and the fun I have with the girls there in our efforts to make everyone fall as much in love with their writer's voice, as we are. I told her of my children, and how we made gingerbread cookies, even though it wasn't nearly Christmas yet, simply because the kids wanted to cut out cookie shapes. She laughed at that, and reminded me of her old recipe for cookies, one my mother and I don't make nearly enough.

"Remember you have to roll them flat. Real flat. You want them really thin. Your mother and you never quite get them thin enough."

And she was right, we didn't. My mother and I didn't come ingrained with that same ever-flowing font of patience that my grandmother had, and is. We'd get that cookie dough as flat as we felt like, even though we could hear her in our mind saying that they weren't ready yet, and roll them flatter. I started to laugh then, and she laughed along with me, the sound filling the empty silence around us. It rose and fell over us, slowly twinkling out, stuck on the breeze and drifting away.

I sat there on that bench and turned to the empty place beside me. My fingers brushed the dead, brown leaves from the seat. Music played again, sweeping through the trees and shaking everything up at the roots, and the world spun around. I laughed again, loud enough to drown out the music. It was laughter laced with tears, and they fell and darkened the wood where my grandmother had sat.

"I miss you Mommom, so much."

Perhaps I'll stay here for a bit. Perhaps I'll make this my home for a time. What is time anyway? It may only be another breath, another heartbeat, and the needle will catch again, and silence will fill a world scented by White Shoulders.

THIS IS AN UPRISING

I need your attention

for just a moment,

a minute,

an ounce of your time

and you better give it

'cause I'll only say this once.

I need you to know

that I'm okay.

I'm alright.

I've settled my accounts

and I know who I am,

and I've accepted that.

I have a firm grip

on my identity,

and what you think of me

is just as true

as what I think of me,

and that's alright.

You hear me?

It's alright,

'cause I can handle

the way you describe me to your mother.

I'm an artist,

a student,

a tutor,

a writer.

I actually read for fun.

I'm a Goddess of the Household Duties:

the Queen of the Laundry,

the Ruler of Dishes,

I can make bread,

fry bacon,

boil eggs,

and bake a cake,

all the while

showing my dominance

over the hills of coffee grounds.

And I'm alright

with the way you talk about me

to all your friends.

"She's a freak in bed,

got an amazing ass,

and gives the best head.

Don't you wish your girlfriend was hot like my,

my sweet,

my baby,

my doll,

my love?"

And all those other sweet,

choke-on-the-sugar

words you spill in my ear at night.

I'm a "cunt,

a bitch,

a whore,

and a slut,"

whenever you're pissed,

and that's alright.

I'll be that,

as long as you get to be

a "douchebag,

an asshole,

a dickhead,

and a bastard."

I'm the Master of Imagination

and I make one hell of a Mother.

So, you promise your own

a herd of screaming,

wailing,

red-faced babies,

and that's alright

'cause I've done it before and

I'll do it again.

Ain't nothing to it!

I'm a taxi driver,

a short order cook,

a night owl,

an instant human,

just add coffee,

an amazing

baby-making machine.

I'm a cow with a pump

hooked to my chest

and I'm feeding the world.

I'm a woman,

a daughter,

a sister,

a mother.

I'm a friend,

an enemy,

a lover,

an ex –

I'm a woman,

so at times

I'm PMS personified.

I've got every limb I need

to kick your ass

and might just have

the strength to do it!

I have been stepped on,

stepped around,

and I'm stepping it up.

I've been trampled,

I've been beaten,

bruised,

and scarred.

I've been raped

and forced,

pushed

and pulled.

I've fallen down

and got back up.

Sometimes, I just laid there

and took it.

I'm weak and frail,

but I'm not porcelain.

I'm girly in ribbons and bows,

but I got a pair of nuts

to make Chuck Norris jealous.

Are you listening to me?

I'm telling you I'm alright.

I'm okay.

I can look in the mirror

and know every day

just who I am

and who you think I am,

and that's alright too.

I am unknown,

uncaring,

unaffected,

unemotional,

and in charge.

I'm the leader of this pack,

the glue that holds the family together,

and I'm only out in the open

screaming at the top of my lungs

when it gets to be too much,

too often.

I don't drink

'cause I've got a low tolerance

and one of them would have me

on a tabletop somewhere,

losing clothes

like I'm losing hair.

I dance like a white chick,

all elbows and knees.

I sing like a wounded cat

and play drums on my steering wheel.

I'm a woman so I can't drive,

can't parallel park

and can't reverse.

I've run into

and away from

and around

mailboxes,

ditches,

people,

responsibilities.

I like language

and can't master my own,

but I'm a true professional

at the Art of Sarcasm.

I say, "I'm fine"

when I'm not,

and "nothing's wrong"

when everything is.

And "whatever" is the equivalent

to a nuclear warhead

landing on your face.

Do you understand me?

'Cause I'm a woman

and I want you to listen

as much as I want to talk.

I'm me.

I'm alright with that.

I'm okay.

I'm stoic.

I can look in the mirror

and I know who I am.

I've been stabbed

and poked

a million times

by needles of every shape

and size.

I treat my body like a canvas

and here I am,

a work of art.

I dye my hair

like I change my underwear.

So you can take

a new girlfriend to bed,

red,

brown,

blonde,

black,

blue,

purple.

Doesn't matter,

I'll be what you want.

It's amazing

what a little

Revlon

Maybelline,

L'Oreal,

Vicadin,

Exlax,

cocktail can do to a woman.

I am *Cosmo*,

Maxim,

Playboy,

and *Good Housekeeping.*

I wear skinny jeans

on my fat days.

I wear pantyhose

to streamline

a beeline

straight to my boobs.

I wear a bra

'cause some man said I should,

even though

I got nothing to put in it.

So I'm thankful for Victoria

and her Secret

gave me something to expose.

I'm a model,

a calendar girl,

a rockstar,

in my mirror with a hairbrush

and I'm belting out the tunes

of punk rock,

oldies,

metal,

and the classics.

I'm a country girl

with an affinity

for hip-hop.

I am tuneless,

tasteless,

careless,

and passionate.

Are you still here?

Hang on,

'cause I've only just begun.

I've just got going,

just got started,

and I'm not there yet.

I'm equipped with high tech

plug-ins.

I've got a vagina,

a pussy,

a cunt,

a hole,

and it's been stabbed,

and poked,

prodded,

and stretched.

It's bled,

and pushed out life.

I've got an attraction

and you can't deny it.

It's dress and silk in the day,

and leather and lace at night.

And I don't get it,

I'm confused,

but I roll with it.

'Cause you want it,

and I can handle it.

I do.

I've seen myself do it.

I am uptight,

upbeat,

upchucking,

and this is an uprising.

This is an acceptance,

of who I am,

and who you make me.

And that's alright.

It's okay.

I'm telling you I can handle it.

I'm allowing,

alluring,

and an illusion.

I am me.

I am woman.

And I'm alright.

DEAR ME, AMEN

What do you want to be when you grow up? Let's color a picture of a police man now. Stay in the lines. You could be a doctor man. An astronaut man. The President man of the United States. Our country tis of thee. I pledge allegiance to the flag. Sweet land of liberty. Under God. Our Father who art in heaven. The B-I-B-L-E , yes that's the book for me. Be nice to your brother, he'll be your best friend some day. He's all you've got. Stop rough-housing. Find your shoes. Sit like a lady. I can do all things through Christ who strengthens me. Your hair looks like an afro. Hallowed be thy name. Tap the rockies. Soup goes in the soup bowls. Ask the fire department for a scholarship. You're going to college. You've got to roll them flatter than that. Smoke Marlboros. What's the matter honey? Talk to me now. You belong to me, always. I won't let you divorce me. Are you the cleaning lady? I'm so hungry. I want you to go in there and do what you're supposed to do. She's lost her fuckin' mind. I'm calling your mother. Please. Please. Please. It's too late. Thy kingdom come. Do it here, or I'll get rid of it myself. How long till we can fuck? I'll never give you a divorce. He has ten days to appeal the decision. Would you like to press charges? Tell me why you tried to end your life. Don't write on the walls. No one will know what happened. Bring the wash out of the bathroom. Do the switch. Get that load of dishes done. Thy will be done. Clean your room. Put the clothes away. Vacuum. Dust. Cinderella. Cinderella. Can you put lotion on my hands? Where's the other baby? Where's your son?

You're not far enough along, go home. Please don't die. The baby is stuck. On earth as it is in heaven. I'm tired, you get her. I lost my job. Are you what I need? Pay attention to me. Pay attention to me. You should get rid of it. I want to be with her. I love you, Red. I never loved you. I just wanted to make sure he got my name. You ruined my life. You did this. You did this. You did this. Give us this day our daily bread. I don't care if he's dying, don't call me. I want to see my son. I want to see my daughter. I just don't have time. I'm broke. Stop trying to steal every penny from me. Fuck you. And forgive us our debts. There's no one to blame but yourself. I shot someone today. Their head just exploded. It was my patrol. I sent him out. I think I love you and I want to show you how much. Follow me. Stay there. Don't move. Women, always plotting something. Shut up. As we have forgiven our debtors. You need to come back to God. Welcome to college. Let's jump right into the syllabus. I don't care if your son is sick; you need to be in class. It's due tonight. It's due tomorrow. It's due yesterday. I'd like to offer you a job. We're going bankrupt. The business went up. He has dementia. I can't handle this. You do it. You do it. You do it. And lead us not into temptation. Get your priorities straight. What do you want to watch? So what are we doing? Are we together? I love you, too. I love you, too. I love you, too. Their my kids. Congrats babe. Get some rest. Non-traditional student. But deliver us from evil. Roll with it, baby. You'll never make money doing that. Why can't you afford it? It's time to renew your food stamp application. Your medical application. Your sliding scale fee paperwork. Do you have time to post? You're so talented. Write what sells. When are you going to move out? For thine is the kingdom. Marry me. We're not ready for a baby. Switch your major and do something that makes money. You still want to marry me? I love you, sweetness. I love you, Shuggie. I love you, Mommy. The power. ¿Cuántos años tienes? No, ¿cuántos años tienes? Forget it. You…¿Cuántos años tienes? And the glory. You rock. You rock hard. I love your characters. No one will ever believe that. For ever and ever. Tell me what's wrong. They need to stop calling you Shuggie. Pay attention to me. Pay attention to me. Pay attention to me. You can be anything you want to be. You can do it all. I'll bury you here one day. Amen.

It Was Winter

It was winter. Frost clung to the grass making it shine as if someone had carelessly scattered precious jewels all over her backwoods, country yard. Amazingly enough, she wasn't even cold; standing out here in her shapeless black dress and peek-a-boo toed, black shoes, it was as if the wind couldn't touch her. Nothing could touch her. She turned and watched the others, dressed in their best. Black dresses, dark suits, clicking heels and purses full of tissues and cigarettes. No one bothered to call her, they knew she'd come. It wasn't as if she could miss this.

Julianna went to the car in silence. She slipped in the backseat, and laid her forehead against the cool window. She counted yellow lines as they whizzed by, so that by the time they had finally arrived, she was dizzy with their flashes of color.

Everyone else went inside, in pairs and groups. Julianna hung back though. She stood against the car and lit a cigarette. Through the small clouds of smoke she watched the parking lot fill up. Everyone's Sunday best was out for display, like some kind of parade of badly dressed, puffy eyed evangelists. She stubbed out her cigarette under her heel, straightened her shoulders and braced herself as memories flooded her. With every step across the parking lot, across the street, up the steps and in the door, images of her daughter slammed in to her.

The nurse handed her a screaming little bundle of angry, red flesh and bright, blue eyes. Julianna cried herself, and as the baby settled in her arms she felt a peace she had never known. She prayed, "Lord, please help me be a good mother."

She stopped and looked both ways across the street, avoiding the other small groups who were headed in the same direction as her. They left her be, thankfully.

Her daughter was up and walking by a year. Her tiny little frame danced under tabletops. She spoke in gibberish and giggles. Occasionally, a few actual words managed to slip between her far spaced, random teeth and her cherry red lips. "Mommy, lub chu."

Standing on the sidewalk, Julianna looked up at the old, white house. It was beautiful, elegant and held no hint of the baggage it carried inside. She wondered if eventually it would turn as ugly on the outside as the emotions that forever crowded its inner rooms.

Julianna had been up all night long. Tylenol and throw up buckets, cool baths and ginger ale. And now she paced the hallways with a sleeping child in her arms. Her daughter was almost too big for this now, but even though her arms were going numb, she still walked with her. She felt the sweat from her daughter leak through and soak her nightshirt. She attempted to lay her down a few times, only to hear her daughter's desperate whine, relent, and go back to her pacing. "God, please help her sleep," Julianna begged in her desperation.

The door opened with a creak of well-used hinges, and she slipped inside after the last little group. It was packed, and for a moment she couldn't breathe. Julianna leaned against the walls, slamming her eyes shut, her chest heaving up and down.

They were sitting at the dinner table, and her daughter was doing better at making faces with the food on her plate, than actually eating any of it. "You have to eat," Julianna reprimanded her again. Her daughter looked up with a set mouth and crinkled eyes, and Julianna braced herself for a temper tantrum. "I don't like meatloaf," and she shoved the plate across the table. It kept on sliding and fell to the floor with a crash. Pieces of plate and food scattered everywhere, and her daughter burst into tears. "I'm sorry. I'm sorry, Mommy. I'm sorry." Julianna took a deep breath, mentally asking God for patience. "Stop crying and come help clean it up, then you can go sit down for a bit. And no TV." Who knew that terrible twos, lasted until they were five?

People avoided her as if she had the plague, which was good, because the last thing she wanted was for all those clinging, sobbing people to touch her. She didn't want their grief hanging over her, joining her own cloud and brewing a storm above her head. She didn't need their tears mixed with her own. Julianna made her way to where the family stood. Her brothers were there, as were her father and mother. They stood in a row to the side of a shining silver casket. The lid was open and Julianna averted her eyes. She didn't look, and couldn't. So she moved to the end of the line, furthest from it, and stood back behind her family. She watched the people move through the line, peek into the casket, and then come and shake hands with the family.

They were climbing in the car, on their way to school. Her daughter had refused to get up this morning, so Julianna had begged, pleaded, yelled and screamed. She'd finally pulled the covers away and peeled her daughter out of bed. "You're going to be late, come on girl." By a miracle alone they made it out the door, but still, as the door closed they watched the bus speed on by. Julianna cursed under her breath, and then ushered her daughter to the car. She strapped her in the car-seat and headed out on the road towards the school.

She overheard one couple discussing with her mother some terrible accident. Julianna only caught bits and pieces, but she couldn't have cared less. Their words meant little to her, and she continued to hang back in her own little world. She let her memories wash over her like waves on the beach, full of salt and gritty sand that bit at her skin, and smoothed away her emotions.

Perhaps it was for this reason that people avoided her. Occasionally, one would look in her direction, but their tear-clouded eyes turned quickly away. No one knew what to say to her, and since she wasn't offering any hints herself, they just avoided the situation completely. One by one, they made their way through the line, and one by one, they walked past her. No one could say it. No one could simply say, "I'm sorry for your loss." They could say it to the grandparents, to the uncles and aunts. However, not a single one had the strength to say it to the mother, to Julianna.

Julianna was lost in her own thoughts when she looked up and realized that everyone was in the process of finding their seats. Her family had already made their way to the first row, though her mother was heading back to a little room in the corner that housed the nursery. A man in black stood a few paces away from Julianna, leaning heavily on the old, wooden pulpit. Books were opened and scattered across the surface. He began to read from Psalms, "The Lord is close to the brokenhearted; he rescues those whose spirits are crushed."

Julianna shrunk back against the wall. The pastor's words slammed into her as if he had sharpened them into a blade and snuck up behind her to dig them between her ribs. She looked at the crowd of people, whose every movement seemed to be pointed straight at her. They threw their stares and fingers out at her in accusation. *It's all her fault. She did this.*

She made her way out of the door and breathed air that was blessedly fresh and free of the overpowering smells of daisies and roses, old lady perfume and grief. It was only about a mile's walk from this old house to the graveyard, and Julianna kicked her feet out of her heels, leaving them there on the sidewalk. Her bare feet padded across the freezing cold blacktop, and she lit another cigarette as she walked.

Her mind was empty, her emotions as scraped, raw and red as the skin on her bare feet had quickly become. The hill that housed the graveyard came into view through the smoke she blew through her lips. Now the pebbles and gravel of the little road ate into her feet, but Julianna relished the slight pain of it. At least, for the moment, she was feeling something. It seemed no time at all before she found the spot where the earth had opened its mouth and lay patient and waiting. The frost had clung here as well, turning the dirt to mud and the grass to bits of tinsel. Tears welled in her eyes, and Julianna gave a moment's thought to laying herself down in it. It would hold her, easily, and why was that? Why had the ground been so greedy as to open so wide a chasm for such a tiny life?

The cars rolled up one at a time in a parade of dark sedans. Their tires crunched across the gravel and woke Julianna from her reverie. With a final look down into that hole, she turned and moved back from the scene to the safety of a huge willow that lay across the little path next to another group of stones. She busied her fingers with plucking the thin leaves from the low-hanging branches while the casket was moved, while the people crushed the tinsel, while the ladies' heels sunk in the mud.

"He will wipe every tear from their eyes, and there will be no more death or sorrow or crying or pain. All these things are gone forever." Julianna turned at the pastor's words and looked at the crowd as it shifted and moved.

The people were leaving, making their way back to the cars. As the dark dresses and coats swayed, she caught a glimpse, there. Julianna leaned forward, straining her head to peek around the moving mass. It thinned, bit by bit, and there, another glimpse. Her feet carried her forward, even as her legs shook. She wrung her hands into knots, tears welling in her eyes. Finally, she was close enough, and there on the last seat she saw her.

The child's dark hair was pulled back in a ponytail, but those random curls she had always had, escaped and tickled across her cheeks and over her ears. She wore her Christmas dress, black with little red roses and a large red bow that tied in the back. Julianna stared at the tiny, patent leather black shoes the kicked back and forth on the seat, scraped and scuffed with white marks. Julianna's mother had her arm wrapped around the young child.

Julianna stepped closer and knelt, her eyes overflowing with tears, before the chair. She reached out and traced the part of the child's hair, and down her cheek. The little girl looked up, and through Julianna. In that moment she was thankful. She was thankful for the grave that lay open behind her, because she now could see who it was meant for. Here, was her child, her sweet little girl. The cold ground was not meant for her daughter. Julianna's hand shook as she cradled her daughter's face, until the little girl shifted and dug her face into the comfort of her grandmother's side. Leaning forward, Julianna kissed her daughter lightly on the back of her head, turned and stepped into the mouth of the earth.

Now, here's a special preview of

the next book in

Laura A. Lord's

collection

HISTORY OF A WOMAN

Available Now

Wake Up a Woman

HISTORY OF A WOMAN

The girls made their way down the winding dirt road, their white dresses flapping gently against their bony knees. They were linked, hand-in-hand, fingers entwined, feet moving in the same rhythm. Two girls became one, melded and meshed until anyone looking saw one set of dark eyes, one little, white dress, one pair of bobby socks and tennis shoes.

So they said, "I need something. Something to make me shine. I look like every other girl. I need to find my fire."

And as one they reached out. They grabbed the electric fence on the side of that dirt road, that border between cow and field, between man and earth, between "we" and "I".

The current shot through them. It made a wide loop through their chest, pumped through their fast-beating heart, coiled in their stomach and shot out of their fingertips with the carefully trimmed and clean nails. It lit up the world and the girls shone bright as a beacon, as the star over Bethlehem, as a lighthouse on a rocky shore, as the perfect edges of a solar eclipse.

Down the road came the old women. Their wrinkled skin and crooked limbs illuminated by the girls. They wore faces carved by worry, haste, and disgust. They wore old housecoats and nightgowns. They wore hats and scarves to cover their hair. They were empty of any embellishment, extravagant in their very own settled ways.

"You'll bring the men!" They yelled at the girls, panic evident in their voices. "You aren't ready."

So the old women gathered. They lifted their skirts and pulled free baskets of laundry, tubs of hot water, dirty dishes, pants and irons, rags and sponges, sides of beef and potatoes with the peels still intact. They lifted their skirts and pulled out the tools of their trade and said, "Learn. What will you do when he asks for the beat biscuits to be made like his mother did?"

But the girls' hands were full of fence and light. So they opened their chest and new arms came out. New hands grew and fumbled around. They took up the laundry, the beef, and the pants. They sewed buttons, washed forks, and punched the dough into the bowl.

When they'd finished, the road beneath them was paved. The black tar radiated heat that made the old women fan themselves as they walked off, mumbling.

"Did it well enough, I suppose."

"Did you see the crease in those pants?"

"Shameful."

The girl's hands stayed full, working past exhaustion. Their light still bright and drawing the young women, who in short day dresses, in pencil skirts and high-heeled shoes, in bangle bracelets and pearl studs, in short trench coats and free-flowing hair came running down the road.

"Stop!" They yelled at the girls. "You'll bring the men. I've seen them. They're coming!"

So the young women gathered around the girls and lifted their skirts. They reached up and pulled out books and paper, maps and pens, musical instruments and sets of oil pastels. They pulled out the new tools and said, "Learn. What will you do when he asks the longitude of Memphis?"

But the girls' hands were full and they couldn't let go of the fence for fear of losing their precious light. So they opened their chest again and more arms sprang free. The hands grabbed at the pages, flipping, turning, devouring every little phrase.

Around them the cows went away. The fields disappeared and a development of postcard picture houses popped up. Picket fences marked the boundaries and basketball hoops stood like sentries at the foot of every driveway. The young women left them, flipping their loose hair.

"Couldn't even find Albuquerque."

"Not a single original thought."

"They tried. They tried."

And so the girls were left with the pressed pants and the peeled potatoes, with the maps of colonies and the stars and stripes, with cups and saucers full of the total percent of the third greatest export of Cyprus.

But the men had seen the light and in their casual time, their easy manner, they passed the old women who dipped their heads to stare at their feet. They passed the young women who stepped back out of the way. They found the girls and dropped their pants. They stood there, flaccid cocks against their thighs and said, "Please me."

Again the girls tried to open their chest, but there was no more room. No room for more arms, more hands and fingers. So the men put their hands on the girls' shoulders and pushed them to their knees. And the girls changed the current. They opened their mouth and gave their fire away. They swallowed the men and made them shine.

Please visit

http://historyofawoman.wix.com/lauraalord

for more information about Laura A. Lord

and her upcoming work

www.ingramcontent.com/pod-product-compliance
Lightning Source LLC
Chambersburg PA
CBHW020645130626
46552CB00003B/1408